The Muddy Puddle

Written by Cynthia Rider
Illustrated by Nicola Evans

It rained and it rained.

See the muddy puddle!

It rained and it rained.
A frog hopped in the
muddy puddle.

It rained and it rained.
A hen pecked in the
muddy puddle.

It rained and it rained.
A dog paddled in the
muddy puddle.

It rained and it rained.
A bird splashed in the
muddy puddle.

It rained and it rained.
A duck swam in the
muddy puddle.

It rained and it rained.
A tractor drove in the
muddy puddle.

It rained and it
rained and...

I jumped in the
muddy puddle!

Guiding a First Read of
The Muddy Puddle

It is important to talk through the book with the child before they read it alone. This prepares them for the way the story unfolds, and allows them to enjoy the pictures as you both talk naturally, using the language they will later encounter when reading. Read them the brief overview, and then follow the suggestions below:

1. Talking through the book
One day, it rained and rained until there was a muddy puddle in the middle of the garden. Some animals and a tractor went in it. Then a girl came along and jumped in the muddy puddle.

Let's read the title: **The Muddy Puddle.**
Turn to page 4. "It rained and it rained.
See the muddy puddle."
Did it keep on raining? Let's see on page 6.
Yes, "It rained and it rained. A frog hopped
in the muddy puddle."
Does he like it there? Let's see who comes
on the next page. Yes, a hen pecked in the
muddy puddle.

Continue through the book, guiding the discussion to fit the text as the child looks at the illustrations.

On page 18, has it stopped raining? No, it hasn't.
Let's turn to the last page. Here a girl comes along
and says, "I jumped in the muddy puddle!"

2. A first reading of the book

Ask the child to read the book independently, pointing carefully under each word (tracking), while thinking about the story. Praise attempts by the child to correct themselves, and prompt them to use their letter knowledge, the punctuation and check the meaning, for example:

> **You said, "A frog jumped in the muddy puddle." That makes sense but check it again carefully. 'Jumped' starts with the letter 'j', doesn't it? What does the third word (hopped) start with? Now try again. Is 'hopped' right? Good.**
>
> **I like the way you corrected it all by yourself. That was excellent checking.**

3. Follow-up activities

The high frequency words in this title are:

a   and   in   it   the

- Select a new high frequency word, and ask the child to find it throughout the book. Discuss the shape of the letters and the letter sounds.
- To memorise the word, ask the child to write it in the air, then write it repeatedly on a whiteboard or on paper, leaving a space between each attempt.

4. Encourage

- Reading the book again – with expression.
- Drawing a picture based on the story.
- Writing one or two sentences using the practised words.

23

START READING is a series of highly enjoyable books for beginner readers. **The books have been carefully graded to match the Book Bands widely used in schools.** This enables readers to be sure they choose books that match their own reading ability.

Look out for the Band colour on the book in our Start Reading logo.

The Bands are:

Pink Band 1A & 1B

Red Band 2

Yellow Band 3

Blue Band 4

Green Band 5

Orange Band 6

Turquoise Band 7

Purple Band 8

Gold Band 9

START READING books can be read independently or shared with an adult. They promote the enjoyment of reading through satisfying stories supported by fun illustrations.

Cynthia Rider lives in the Peak District of Derbyshire and often finds inspiration for her stories in the countryside around her. She particularly enjoys writing for young children and encouraging their love of reading.

Nicola Evans works as a freelance illustrator in a small village on the south coast of England, where she lives with her husband and three-year-old daughter. She loves illustrating for children, helping to bring books alive with her characters and colours.